Hattie Baked a Wedding Cake

by **Toby Speed**

illustrated by **Cathi Hepworth**

G. P. Putnam's Sons   New York

Text copyright © 1994 by Toby Speed
Illustrations copyright © 1994 by Catherine Hepworth
All rights reserved. This book, or parts thereof, may not be reproduced
in any form without permission in writing from the publisher.
G. P. Putnam's Sons, a division of The Putnam & Grosset Group,
200 Madison Avenue, New York, NY 10016.
G. P. Putnam's Sons, Reg. U.S. Pat. & Tm. Off.
Published simultaneously in Canada.
Printed in Hong Kong by South China Printing Co. (1988) Ltd.
Type set in Windsor Light

Library of Congress Cataloging-in-Publication Data
Speed, Toby. Hattie baked a wedding cake/by Toby Speed;
illustrated by Cathi Hepworth. p. cm.
Summary: Hattie accidentally bakes into a wedding cake a number of
items vital to the wedding and must find a way to get them out again.
[1.Cakes—Fiction. 2. Baking—Fiction. 3. Weddings—Fiction.]
I. Hepworth, Catherine, ill. II. Title. PZ7.S746115Hat
1994 [E]—dc20   91-30888 CIP AC
ISBN 0-399-22342-8
1 3 5 7 9 10 8 6 4 2
First Impression

For Vanessa, Kate, and Zoe, with love
—T.S.

For Mom & Dad and Chuck & Dee...
thanks for all your help.
—C.H.

For the garden wedding of the cobbler and the cook, Fran brought the flowers,
Bert brought the streamers, and Jill brought a hundred red balloons.

And Hattie baked the wedding cake. She beat in flour. She beat in eggs.

She beat in raisins. She beat in nuts. She beat and beat and beat the batter.

And then, because she was beating so hard, some other things got

mixed in, too. The wind in the wind chimes, a pair of specs,

chamber music from a string quartet,

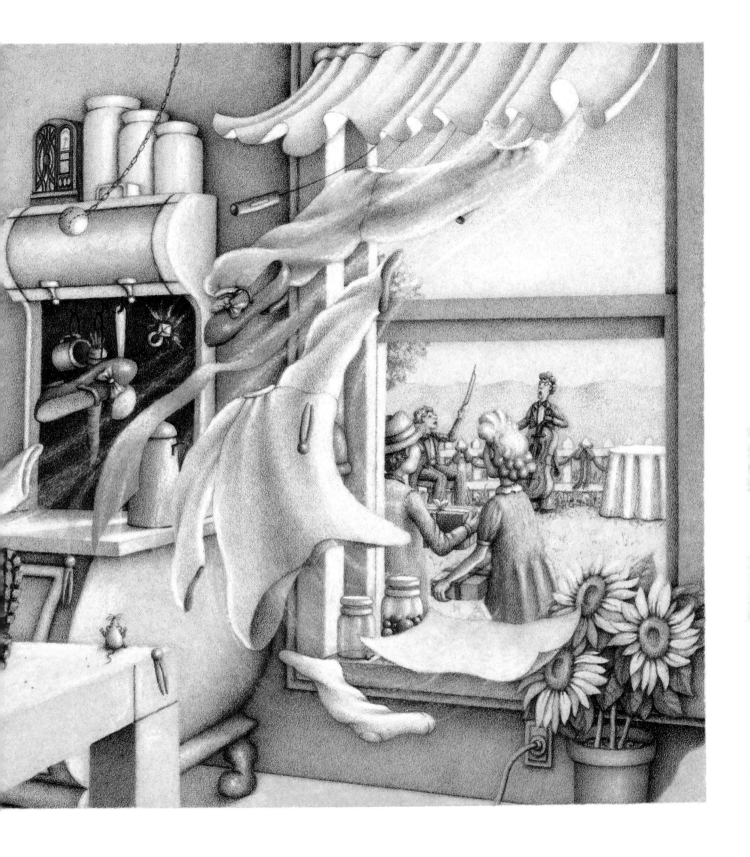

two socks from the line, an antique ring, some dancing shoes,

three stray sunbeams, a rosebud tripping down the street,

and a kiss someone blew that missed a cheek—all went into the cake.

Hattie beat the batter and the batter got bigger. Soon she had
an enormous bowlful. It was too big for the pan, so she poured it
in the washtub. It was too big for the washtub, so she baked it
in the tuba.

"What a fine cake to be in a wedding," said Hattie.

And so it was.

After it cooled, she carried it to the wedding.

But when she got to the garden...

What a mix-up!

The wind chimes were silent, the judge had to squint, the musicians
could not play a note, the groom had no socks, the usher no ring,
the flower girl cried for her shoes, the sky was dark on the faraway side,

the bouquet of roses was missing a bud, and there wasn't a kiss for the bride.

"We can't have a wedding without a kiss," said the judge.

The bride only cried.

"Look!" shouted the groom. "The kiss is in the cake!"

For a minute nobody moved. Everyone stared at the kiss in the cake.

"I got it in there," said Hattie at last. "So I will get it out."

Hattie cut a slice. The kiss wouldn't budge. She climbed up
the tuba and dug in with a spoon. The kiss wouldn't budge.

Finally she blew into the mouthpiece

Whoomph!

Out flew the cake, straight across the garden. And...

...out went the wind, out went the specs, out went the chamber music,

out went the socks, out went the antique ring, out went the dancing shoes,

out went the sunbeams, out went the rosebud, and out went the kiss—

out into the middle of the wedding. The bride sniffed and dried her tears.

Then the wind chimes tinkled, the judge found his specs, the string quartet played a lively tune, the groom tied his shoes, the flower girl

danced, all the guests admired the ring, the sky lit up, the rosebud bloomed, and the bride and groom kissed, and kissed again.

"What a fine wedding to be in a cake," said Hattie.

And so it was.